CW00848339

THE HUNGRY HORRISS

by Marc Bolton and Adrian D. Lewis

This book is dedicated with much love to Milo, Otis, Enzo, Aidan and Abby,
without whom life just wouldn't be the same,
(or quite as chaotic!).

P.S.

Don't forget to check out the competition page at the end of this book and you
could win yourself an original signed poster for your bedroom wall.

And YOU get to choose which page you want as your poster!

Copyright © Marc Bolton and Adrian D. Lewis 2019. All rights reserved.
ISBN: 9781091466791

If you ever meet a Horriss, and I rather doubt that you will, but if you did, the first thing you would notice was its size.

If you imagine a little round body, about the size of a tennis ball, that's been covered in thick black fur and had two little green arms and two little green legs stuck on it, with two of the beadiest little yellow eyes blinking somewhere in the middle, then you're pretty much imagining a Horriss.

1

The second thing you would have noticed is its smell. No matter where they've been, a Horriss always smells like a wet dog that's been rolling in cabbage. This is because they spend much of their early lives jumping from puddle to puddle across boggy marshlands and never bothering to dry themselves properly.

There aren't many who can stand downwind of a Horriss for too long, that's for sure.

And the third thing you would notice is that a Horriss is one of the most disagreeable creatures you could ever meet, always grumbling or griping about something.

A boy in Finland said he saw one smile once after his grandfather walked into a tree, but this has never been confirmed.

It was most probably just breaking wind. Horrisses are notoriously gassy and fart constantly throughout the day and night. It's one of the few things that seems to to amuse them.

The good news though is that although they might be noisy and repulsive, only the Stinky Horriss's expulsions are actually dangerous, having once knocked out an entire village with one almighty guff.

PARP

Each and every Horriss is born with a gift. And when I say 'born', I do of course mean coughed up like a slimey furball and left to jump around in bog puddles until it gets bored and wanders off.

Each gift is unique to that particular Horriss and once discovered, becomes the name by which it is known forever more.

A Horriss's gift is its ability to do something to such an extreme that us humans can barely believe it's possible.

Sometimes the gift is really obvious...

...like the Thirsty Horriss, who popped up out of a bog and within five minutes had drunk it completely dry...

7

...or the Sleepy Horriss, who stayed asleep for 227 years, woke up to drink a glass of water, then went back to sleep for another 322 years...

YAAWWWN

... or the Hearing Horriss, who rang the Stinky Horriss a thousand miles away to let it know, "**I heard that.**"

9

Then there's this little fellow, the Hungry Horriss.

The Hungry Horriss is a remarkable creature, although you wouldn't know it to look at it.

It can eat more in an hour than you or I could eat in a year. It never gets fat and never gets full, and if it finishes its dinner and can't be bothered to wash up (which is every time), it just eats the knife and fork. And the plates, the chairs, the table, the carpet, curtains, wallpaper, even the walls. In fact anything it can get its hungry little hands on.

11

Nobody knows how old the Hungry Horriss is, but to give you some idea, one day it woke up and decided it wanted Brontosaurus for breakfast.

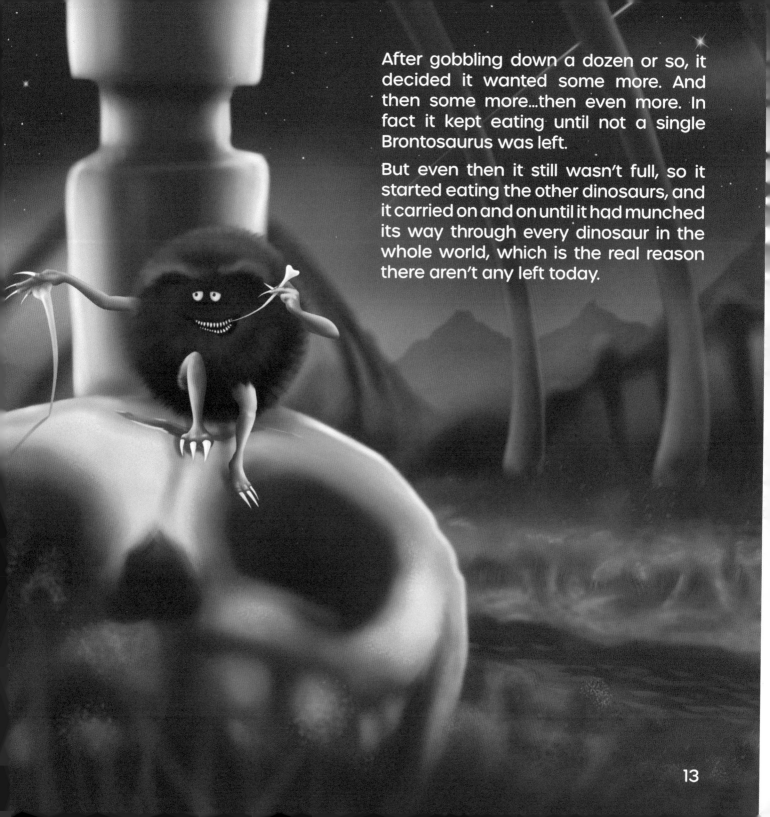

After gobbling down a dozen or so, it decided it wanted some more. And then some more...then even more. In fact it kept eating until not a single Brontosaurus was left.

But even then it still wasn't full, so it started eating the other dinosaurs, and it carried on and on until it had munched its way through every dinosaur in the whole world, which is the real reason there aren't any left today.

We know this because if you look at any dinosaur bone under a microscope, from a T-Rex to a Mammoth, you'll find it has tiny little teeth marks all over it. That was the Hungry Horriss.

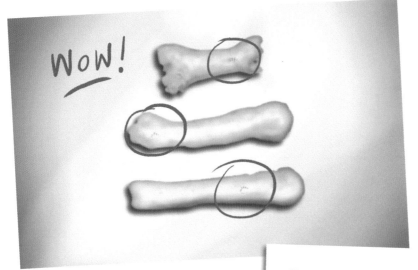

EXHIBIT 1453A

Velociraptor Bones

Age: 73 million years

Discovered 1953

EXHIBIT 547923431A

Elephant Bones

Age: Unknown

Discovered 2014

The same thing happened to the Dodo (which is pronounced Doh Doh and not Do Do. That's something else entirely).

Once, while it was on holiday, the Hungry Horriss felt a bit peckish and saw a lovely plump Dodo walking in the woods. It gobbled it up and....well, you can guess the rest.

It is even said that the Earth used to have a lot more land, hardly any sea at all, until the Hungry Horriss got a taste for soil. Thankfully, six weeks later, it decided it wanted a change, otherwise we'd all be living in boats and moles would be in a proper pickle.

Naturally, people began to worry about the Hungry Horriss's appetite. What if it woke up one morning and fancied eating humans?!

It was decided that something must be done. So, the cleverest men in the world got together and, after a great deal of bickering and arguing (mostly about who was the cleverest), they thought of a cunning plan to catch the Hungry Horriss.

First though they had to find it, and finding a Horriss is a difficult business. With their springy little legs they can cover great distances very quickly.

The only thing the cleverest men in the world knew for sure was that when it got a taste for something, the Hungry Horriss would usually eat it all up until there wasn't any left.

So they decided to watch for things mysteriously disappearing, and it wasn't long before they noticed that tigers were becoming very scarce in Africa.

Dad, are Africa's tigers really gone?

eek

17

Hurrying over there, they proceeded to catch a tiger, and just as the African sun was setting, they put it in a cage... and waited.

After waiting for a couple of days, one of the men heard a very strange noise.

It sounded for all the world like a tiny tummy rumbling.

Before anyone knew what was happening, the tiger let out a mighty roar and all the men ran for the cage.

After a great deal of running around and bumping into each other, one of the men held up his sack and shouted "I've got it!".

All the other men rushed over and put the first sack into another sack, then those sacks into another sack, and another sack, and so on until the Hungry Horriss was inside 50 strong leather sacks. "Hurrah!" everyone cried.

But the celebrations were short-lived, for two reasons. Firstly, it was noticed that the Hungry Horriss had actually eaten the tiger, which was a shame as it turned out to be the very last one, and to this day there are still no tigers in Africa.

Secondly, from deep within the sacks, the men could hear a sound. A chewing sound. A chomping sound. A munching, crunching, lunching sound. The Hungry Horriss was eating his way out!

"To the box!!" cried the cleverest men in the world, and the bundle of sacks was rushed over to a large shiny box and dropped inside, resulting in some very loud grumbling indeed.

As the last rays of the sun disappeared over the horizon, the lid was locked shut. At that exact moment, the last sack vanished into its gobbly little mouth and there sat the Hungry Horriss.

Blinking its beady little green eyes, it stood up on its little green legs and walked over to one side of the box. Putting a little green hand out, it ran it slowly over the smooth, shiny surface. Then, without warning, it bared its fearsomely sharp teeth and tried to bite the box.

Nothing happened. It tried again. Not a scratch.

It tried one last time, and then something amazing happened. It broke a tooth!

This was especially amazing when you consider that stones, bones and black plastic phones had all disappeared into its mouth at one time or another, yet this strange shiny box had just broken one of its favourite teeth!

You see, the box was made of diamond, the hardest thing in the world and even the Hungry Horriss can't bite through diamond, so it sat back down feeling very puzzled indeed.

The cleverest men in the world didn't wait around to see what would happen next.

22

The diamond box was placed on a giant seesaw at the bottom of a cliff, while high above, the clever men's hapless henchmen began pushing a huge boulder towards the cliff edge.

They pushed and pushed and heaved and pushed, until eventually the boulder fell off and went hurtling down, smashing into the seesaw at over eight hundred miles an hour.

In the blink of an eye the diamond box, with the Hungry Horriss still trapped inside, shot up, high into the sky.

BOING GC

SMASH

23

Higher and higher it went, past the birds, past the clouds and off into space, while far below, the cleverest men in the world all patted themselves on the back for a job well done and went off to tell their friends how they, and they alone, had thought of the idea.

Meanwhile, the diamond box, which had been travelling through space for a very long time, suddenly, and without any warning, collided with a comet.

By pure chance, the comet was also made of diamond, which is why the diamond lock on the diamond box suddenly broke, the lid popped wide open, and the Hungry Horriss found itself hurtling towards a huge round rock, clinging on for dear life.

The box landed with a soft thwump and the Hungry Horriss rolled gently out, finding itself in a very strange place indeed. No trees, no grass, no anything, just grey rocks and dust as far as its beady little eyes could see. It was on the Moon!

It was just about to start the biggest grumble of its life, when it stopped. And sniffed. And sniffed again. What was that delicious smell? It was everywhere!

It picked up a moonrock and had a nibble. Its beady little eyes almost popped out of its black furry head. It was DELICIOUS! It ate the rock. Then it picked up another and ate that too. And another. And another. Moonrock, as it turned out, was the most scrumptious thing it had ever tasted!

Without wasting another moment, the Hungry Horriss began stuffing moonrocks into its mouth as fast as it could.

After an hour there was a crater the size of a house, but it didn't stop there. Oh no. A day later there was a canyon two miles deep and ten miles long, but it didn't stop there. A week later a quarter of the Moon was gone and still it kept chomping.

After just two weeks, more than half of the Moon had disappeared into its greedy little tummy, but still it wanted more!

On and on it went, chomping and chewing, until finally, a month later, it looked down at its little green feet and found it was standing on the very last, very teeny weeny piece of moonrock.

Now you or I would've probably stopped eating then, but not the Hungry Horriss. Without a moment's thought it picked up the last piece of moonrock and gobbled it down.

Gone! The entire Moon!

So there it was, floating around in space, without a scrap of food for miles. Doomed to starve.

Or so it thought.

You see, you can eat a tree, or a dinosaur's knee, and nobody notices...but an entire Moon? Well that's a different story.

The Moon is big. The Moon is huge. The Moon is going to be missed. There was now a space in space, and you can't have a space in space, especially not a Moon-sized one.

It's just not allowed.

The very next day, the Hungry Horriss felt an odd sensation in its tummy. It started as a tremble, then grew into a grumble, before it grew and grew into a full-scale rumble.

And as if that wasn't bad enough, the Hungry Horriss felt its tummy start to swell up.

Bigger and bigger it became, rounder and rounder it stretched, until the Hungry Horriss thought it would surely burst. And then it did.

Well, kind of...

With the loudest "BURP!!!" anyone has ever heard, the Hungry Horriss watched as the entire Moon came tumbling out of its mouth and settled back into place in the Moon-shaped space. Exactly as it had been just a month ago, before the Hungry Horriss had started munching it.

The Hungry Horriss couldn't believe its beady little eyes! It felt so happy! And then it felt something else.

35

A pang. A hunger pang. With no Moon inside it, the Hungry Horriss's belly felt hungrier than ever. "I wonder..." it thought, and picking up a moonrock it carefully nibbled one corner. It was still absolutely delicious!!

In an instant, the Hungry Horriss began eating the Moon all over again. On and on it ate until once again, a month later, it had eaten the lot. And just as before, a day after it had gobbled up the last piece, out burped the Moon and the whole thing started all over again.

The Hungry Horriss is still up there, munching away, and it couldn't be happier. In fact, if you look up at the Moon every now and again, you can see how much it's eaten; sometimes a little, sometimes a lot. Where it puts it all nobody knows, but it certainly is a very Hungry Horriss!

THE END.

WIN A SIGNED ORIGINAL HUNGRY HORRISS POSTER PRINT!!

As you now know, the Hungry Horris cannot eat diamond, so to celebrate the Earth not being gobbled up, we've hidden five very special diamonds in the pages of the book that look just like this one...

To enter our competition to WIN one of TEN signed ORIGINAL Hungry Horriss posters, find all five diamonds and go to the Hungry Horriss web site (address below) and tell us in TEN WORDS or less, the page numbers and roughly whereabouts on each page they are hidden.

And here's the best bit. You get to choose which page of this book you would like as your poster!

Please note, you can only enter if you purchased the book (digital or print), and you can only enter once (anything else would be greedy!).

All ten winners will be announced on the website and we would love it if, when you've received your poster, you could take a picture of yourself holding it, send it to us, and we'll publish it on our website (with your permission of course).

Go online now to enter the competition:

www.thehungryhorriss.com/win

(and please be sure to read our terms and conditions while you're there.)

HAPPY HUNTING!

COMING SOON: LOTS MORE ADVENTURES WITH LOTS MORE HORRISSES!

Horrisses have been on the Earth for a very long time...longer than people, longer than animals, longer even than the dinosaurs. They've always been there, scurrying around in the shadows, watching everything we do...and we think it's time we learned a little bit more about them!

So if you enjoyed The Hungry Horriss, keep an eye out for the next amazing Horriss adventure... coming soon!!!

About the authors

Marc (who writes the words) and Adrian (who draws the pictures) are two dedicated Dads who decided not to grow up. They tried it, as everyone does, but found it to be highly overrated, so they now spend their time dreaming up stories to inspire their children's imaginations, which is much more fun.

The Hungry Horriss is the first story they've shared with the rest of the world, and they very much hope that you like it.

20530586R00024

Printed in Great Britain
by Amazon